and the Missing Sausages

Collins
YELLOW
STORYBOOK

Other Yellow Storybooks by Pat Thomson

Superpooch

and in the Jets series

Messages
Jacko
Rhyming Russell
Lost Property

SUPERPOOCH
and the
Missing Sausages

Pat Thomson
Illustrated by Mike Gordon

CollinsChildren'sBooks
An Imprint of HarperCollinsPublishers

373107

First published in Great Britain by
CollinsChildren'sBooks 1996

3 5 7 9 8 6 4 2

CollinsChildren'sBooks is a division of
HarperCollins*Publishers* Ltd,
77-85 Fulham Palace Road,
Hammersmith, London W6 8JB

Text copyright © Pat Thomson 1996
Illustrations copyright © Mike Gordon 1996

The author and illustrator assert the moral right to be
identified as the author and illustrator of the work.

Printed and bound in Great Britain
by HarperCollins Manufacturing Ltd, Glasgow

ISBN Hardback 0 00 185620 0
Paperback 0 00 675109 1

CONTENTS

1. Superpooch and the Missing
   Sausages   7

2. Trouble in the Toyshop   39

SUPERPOOCH AND THE MISSING SAUSAGES

Chapter 1

This is a little house, in a little street, in the little town of Wittering. There is nothing special about it.

Maybe, maybe not.

This is Mrs May's dog who lives there. He has long ears, a stumpy tail and sleepy eyes. Nothing special about him.

Maybe, maybe not.

They say his name is Poochie. Sometimes it is. Sometimes it isn't.

This is Chatwin, the cat.
Chatwin is a cat who knows the
town. She knows everything that
goes on.

No maybes. She *knows*.
She is the one who knows the
secret of Poochie's two names.
Sleepy Poochie is really
SUPERPOOCH!

Chatwin was not sitting on Mrs May's garden wall as usual. Poochie lay waiting for her and dreaming. He had one eye open and one eye shut.

A big dog walked along the road. He stopped outside Mrs May's house. He stared into the garden. Poochie noticed his bright red collar.

"Hi, Squashy Nose," sneered the dog.

"I beg your pardon?" Poochie replied.

"You've got a face like a fishcake," said the dog.

Poochie was very surprised. "You
are a rude dog," he answered.
"What is the matter with you?"

"Nothing's the matter with me, Floppy Ears," laughed the rude dog. "It's you who looks like something the cat dragged in." He barked loudly and walked away.

"What a cheek," said Poochie. "What a nasty dog." He stared after it. Suddenly, he heard a voice.

"Poochie." It was Chatwin. She stood on Mrs May's wall lashing her tail. Beside her stood a very small kitten. It was Min, Chatwin's youngest cousin.

"We need you," Chatwin said.
"Something terrible has
happened."

Chapter 2

Chatwin jumped down from the wall. "Poochie, it's awful. Something very important is missing."

"Something important?"
Poochie opened both eyes. "Is it
the Queen's crown?"

Chatwin shook her head.
"Is it Mrs May's purse?"

Chatwin shook her head again.

"Far worse. It's the sausages for dinner."

"My dinner?" Poochie stood up.

"No, not yours."
Poochie sat down.

"The sausages belong to
Mrs Wood of 14 Cherry Road.
Min belongs to her too."
Poochie closed his eyes again.
"Sausages come and sausages go,"
he said. "That's the nature of
sausages."

"Bless my little white socks!" exclaimed Chatwin. "You don't understand. Mrs Wood thinks Min stole the sausages. She shouted at her."

"Did you take the sausages Min?" asked Poochie sternly.

NO

"No," mewed Min sadly. "It was a big, big dog. He came right into the kitchen. I couldn't stop him.

He was wearing a red collar."

"A red collar?" Poochie stood up
again. He looked taller. "Take me
to 14 Cherry Road," he said.

Chapter 3

Poochie, Chatwin and Min ran along the pavements until they reached 14 Cherry Road. They stopped outside the gate, under the lamppost.

They saw a garden with a rabbit hutch. The hutch stood under an open window. The back door was also open. From it they heard loud voices.

There was a woman's voice. That was Mrs Wood. She sounded cross. There was a girl's voice. That was her daughter, Katie. She sounded upset.

"Min can't have taken the sausages," Katie was saying. "She's only little."

"She's big enough to eat your dad's dinner, it seems," Mrs Wood answered. "That kitten was alone in the kitchen. I've had to buy more sausages."

"It wasn't me." Min crouched down and put her tail over her eyes. She was crying in a thin little voice.

"Bless my little white socks," sighed Chatwin. "What now?"

"One moment," said Poochie and he ran behind the lamppost. There was a cry of '**BONES AND BISCUITS**'.

Min looked up. She saw a big strong dog, with bright fierce eyes. He swept round the lamppost, his long ears straight out like the wings of an aeroplane.

"**SUPERPOOCH** will help
you, little kitten," said the dog.
"Follow me."

All three of them ran into the garden. Superpooch turned his laser eyes on the house. He could see straight through the wall.

"Yes. I can see Mrs Wood and Katie arguing in the hall. The kitchen door is shut but I shall look in."

"Ha ha!" said Superpooch. "Just watch that open window. It's the kitchen window. Now we shall see the sausage thief."

Chapter 4

Chatwin and Min waited, watching the window all the time. Suddenly, a big dog jumped out of the window. He stood on the top of the rabbit hutch. He had a string of sausages in his mouth… and he wore a red collar!

The dog saw Min and grinned nastily. "Hi there, Furry Features," he said. "Guess who's going to get the blame again?"

There was a whirring noise
overhead. There was a cry of
'BONES AND BISCUITS'
and a shadow swooped over them.

"Don't speak with your mouth
full," boomed Superpooch.

The dog's mouth dropped open.
Superpooch seized the string of
sausages. He slipped them through
the red collar and dragged the dog
to the back door. Superpooch
looked big and strong. The dog
with the red collar now looked
quite ordinary. Min didn't feel
frightened any more.

Superpooch started to bark.
Chatwin started to yowl. Min
managed an excited little mew.

Mrs Wood came to the back door.
When she saw the sausages, she
started to yell. "Horrible dog! Flea
bag! Hairy monster!"

"How does it feel to be called names, Fishcake Face?" asked Superpooch. The dog with the red collar ran out of the garden, his tail between his legs.

Mrs Wood scooped up Min. "What horrible dogs," she declared. "Of course it wasn't you Min. I think those nasty dogs stole the sausages."

Superpooch didn't mind being blamed. He had saved little Min. "Win some, lose some," he said.

"Let's go home, horrible dog," laughed Chatwin. "Mrs Wood thinks you are a hairy monster. Mrs May thinks you are her Poochie. But I know you are SUPERPOOCH!"

TROUBLE IN THE TOYSHOP

Chapter 1

This is Mrs May in the toyshop.
She is buying a toy for her niece's
new baby.

This is Mrs May's Poochie. He lies waiting. His eyes are closed. An ordinary dog on an ordinary day.

Maybe, maybe not.

Mrs May loves to talk. Today, however, she is listening. Mrs Wake, who owns the toyshop, is worried.

"I can't understand it," she says. "Every morning there are some toys missing."

"A break-in?" asks Mrs May.
"I don't know," says Mrs Wake.

"You see, the doors are still locked when I get to the shop. The windows are not broken. It's a mystery."

Poochie's eyes are still closed but he lifts one ear. He is listening too.

"So no one goes in and no one comes out, but the toys disappear.

Very strange," says Mrs May.

"I don't know what to think," sighs Mrs Wake.

Poochie didn't know what to think either. Later, he discussed it with his friend Chatwin.

"I don't like it Chatwin. I don't like mysteries."

"Bless my little white socks," said Chatwin. She licked her whiskers. "It seems to me that you could solve this mystery. We could do it tonight. Shall we meet at midnight?"

She smiled her cat smile. She knew a secret. Poochie was not always Mrs May's sleepy dog.

He was sometimes something quite different.

"I see," said Poochie. "You think this is a case for **SUPERPOOCH!**"

Chapter 2

That night, Chatwin moved through the town without a sound. Poochie padded along just as quietly. It was raining. They walked down dark alleys. They walked past brightly-lit shop windows. Chatwin stopped once.

"Ssh!" she hissed and slipped
into a dark doorway. Poochie
followed. Two tall policemen
walked by. They saw no one else.

Then they reached a shop which had a striped canopy. Chatwin looked up at it. It said WAKE'S TOYS in big letters. The street was empty and the shop was dark.

Chatwin looked carefully at every window. They were all tightly shut.

Poochie looked at every inch of the door. "No one has tried to get in here," he said.

"Bless my little white socks," said Chatwin, looking nervous. "It couldn't be a ghost could it?"

"Of course not, my dear Chatwin," answered Poochie. "There will be a clue of some sort. Keep searching."

"You are right!" said Chatwin. She sounded excited. "Look here!"

Poochie looked at the bottom of the wall, near a drain pipe. The pipe went through the wall to the inside. "The brickwork has been scratched loose here," he said. "There is quite a big hole." Poochie sniffed. "Do you smell what I smell?" he asked.

"Pooh!" exclaimed Chatwin. "Rats!"

"Excuse me," said Poochie.

The next moment, Chatwin heard a cry of '**BONES AND BISCUITS**'. Round the lamppost soared a big, strong **SUPERPOOCH**.

"To business," he cried.

Chapter 3

As Superpooch and Chatwin looked at the hole, they heard something. The sound was coming from the drainpipe.

WHISPER . . WHISPER .

There were bumps and bangs.

BUMP! BANG!

There were squeaks and squeals.

SQUEAK! SQUEAL!

There were whispers and words.

Some of the words were rather rude.

"It's them," whispered Chatwin. "It's the rotten river rats. What are they doing?"

Superpooch turned his laser eyes on to the brick wall. He was looking into the toyshop. It was a disgraceful scene. Toys and boxes were scattered everywhere.

Young rats scampered up the shelves. Old rats chewed their way into boxes.

One rat jumped on a teddy's tummy to make it squeak.

Two others sat in a train set as if they owned it. A young rat knocked a bag of marbles off a high shelf.

The marbles scattered all over the floor. The rats skidded and bumped. That explained the rude words.

On the counter stood the Boss. The big rat had a necklace on his tail. He was holding a doll by its golden hair. Another rat had the doll by its leg.

"Let go," snarled the Boss. "It's mine." He took off the long, golden hair and put it on his own head. He sat there smiling and looking silly.

Superpooch sighed. "Just listen," he said to Chatwin.

Chatwin put her ear to the drainpipe. The rats were singing.

Policemen better stay awake,
For what we want,
we go and take.
Hard luck, little girls and boys,
It's the rotten rats which
get the toys.

All the rats laughed. They were very pleased with themselves.

"I think we should teach them a lesson," said Superpooch softly. He smiled. "What did you say about ghosts, Chatwin?"

Chapter 4

Inside the shop, the rats were singing loudly.

"Policemen better stay awake—"

"What was that?" One rat sat up and twitched his whiskers.

"I can't hear anything," said the Boss.

"For what we want—"

"Ssh! Ssh! I can hear it too!"
There was a sound like a giant breathing.
Then "Whooooooo", a strange, hollow noise.

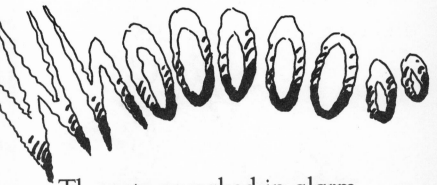

The rats squeaked in alarm.
"Whooooooo. I see you all." The voice boomed round the shop. It came from nowhere. The rats huddled together.

"Whooooooo. I see the golden-haired one especially."

Whoooooooooo...

The Boss snatched the doll's wig off and put it on the next rat's head. He was quite small and disappeared under it.

Superpooch laughed down the drainpipe. He couldn't help it. He quickly changed his laugh into a horrible cackle.

"Save us, save us!" cried the rats, running in all directions. The next moment, they were fighting each other to get out through the hole in the wall.

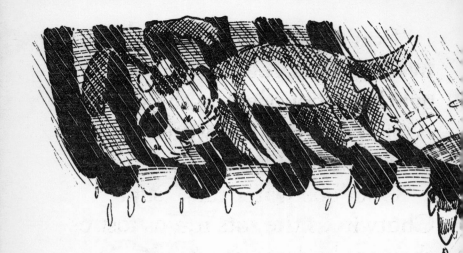

Chatwin jumped out of the way. Superpooch zoomed up on to the shop's canopy. The rats scrambled out and stood shaking under the lamppost.

Superpooch looked down on them. They still could not see him.

"Don't come back," he moaned in his ghost's voice. Then, very gently he bounced on the canopy. A big puddle of rainwater poured down, all over the rats.

"Goodbye water rats," said Chatwin as the rats ran as fast as they could down the road.

"Mystery solved," said Superpooch. "Let's go home."

"I knew you would solve the mystery," said Chatwin. "After all, you may be Mrs May's Poochie but, bless my little white *ghostly* socks, I know you are also **SUPERPOOCH!**"